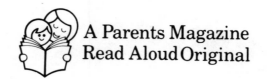

I'd Like To Be

by Steven Kroll
pictures by Ellen Appleby

PARENTS MAGAZINE PRESS
NEW YORK

For Anita and Jay Kaufman,
who are—S.K.

To Jana Bailey—E.A.

Library of Congress Cataloging-in-Publication Data
Kroll, Steven.
I'd like to be.
Summary: A child imagines solving various
problems by being a clock, a doctor, a duck,
and other identities, before deciding that
being "me" is the best of all.
[1. Imagination—Fiction. 2. Identity—
Fiction] I. Appleby, Ellen, ill. II. Title.
PZ7.K9225Id 1987   [E]   86-25215
ISBN 0-8193-1141-3

I'd Like To Be

When I'm at the supermarket
and I can't reach my favorite cookies

and Mom gets them for me
but says I can't eat them
until after dinner...

then I'd like to be a GIANT CLOCK
and move my hands
quickly past dinner time.

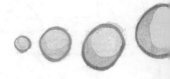

When Dad burns his finger on the stove

and Mom is sneezing
because she caught a cold

and my tummy hurts
because I ate too much…

then I'd like to be a DOCTOR
and make everyone feel better.

Sometimes when it's really raining
and I have to wear my raincoat
and boots and hat all tied up tight...

then I'd like to be a DUCK
with nothing but the feathers on my back.

When my baby sister is grumpy
and I can't find my favorite doll

and Dad is groaning because the cat spilled the laundry soap...

then I'd like to be a CLOWN
and make everyone laugh!

When my big brother sneaks up behind me
and shouts, "Boo!"

or jumps out of his closet
wearing his skeleton suit...

then I'd like to be a MONSTER
and scare him back.

When I pet the rabbits
at the children's zoo

or see the squirrels in the park
or watch the birds in the air...

then I'd like to be REALLY SMALL
so I could get to know them better.

When I'm lying in bed in the dark
and my bureau turns into
a bear wearing a hat
and goblins are playing in the corner...

then I'd like to be QUEEN of them all
and order them back where they came from.

When I get soap in my eyes
and it hurts
and Mom says I've squeezed

too much toothpaste
and asks why I forgot
to wash behind my ears...

then I'd like to be a CAT
who just licks herself clean.

Thinking about all the things I could be is lots of fun.

But when I draw a really good picture

or learn how to tie my shoes

or make a new friend in the park...

then I just like to be ME.
And that is the best of all!

About the author

Steven Kroll explains how he got started on *I'd Like To Be:* "There have been many occasions in my life when I've wanted to be a clown, a monster, a duck, or a doctor, and just as many when I've liked being me. Once, when a very mean-looking person was coming down the street and I was pretending to be a GIANT, I thought: There must be a book in all this. So I dashed home and began *I'd Like To Be.*"

Steven Kroll is the author of thirty-five books for children, including *Pigs In The House, Otto, The Goat Parade,* and *Dirty Feet* for Parents. He lives in New York City.

About the artist

Like the little girl in the story, **Ellen Appleby** has a vivid imagination. "Illustrating *I'd Like To Be* was a lot of fun because it gave me the chance to fantasize, which is especially important to young children. Kids just starting to explore the world around them are often frustrated by events they can't control. So they devise their own imaginative solutions to give themselves a sense of power over their environment. After all, who wouldn't want to be a duck on a rainy day? Just think—you'd never have to carry an umbrella again!"

Ellen Appleby has illustrated many children's books, including *Pets I Wouldn't Pick* and *One Little Monkey* for Parents.